HOOT

HOOT

Jane Hissey

RED FOX

For Susan, Mark, Laurie and Gina

It was the middle of the night and all the toys should have been fast asleep. But Little Bear was wide awake.

He leaned over and tugged at Rabbit's ear. 'Wake up,' he whispered. 'I heard a funny noise.'

'What sort of noise?' muttered Rabbit, sleepily.

'Well, first there was a thump and then a *Whooo*,' said Little Bear. 'Do you think it was a ghost?'

'Probably just the wind outside,' said Rabbit, sitting up and staring into the darkness.

Then they both heard the noise.

Whooo.

'It doesn't really sound like the wind, does it?' said Little Bear, nervously.

Without warning, a white shape drifted past the bed. Rabbit and Little Bear dived under the bedclothes.

'What was *that?*' whispered Little Bear.

'I'm not sure,' said Rabbit. 'Has it gone?'

'I daren't look,' said Little Bear, with his head still covered by the sheet. 'I'll wake Bramwell.'

He wriggled along under the bedclothes and shook Bramwell's paw. 'Wake up,' he whispered. 'There's something in the room. It's whizzing about and saying *Whooo*.'

'Wind, I expect,' said Bramwell. 'Why are you both hiding?'

'We *saw* it,' said Rabbit, 'but we didn't want it to see *us*.'

By now, all the toys were wide awake.

'It's the middle of the night,' grumbled Duck. 'What are you all doing?'

'We saw something white whizz past the bed,' said Little Bear.

'And I suppose it said *Whooo*,' said Duck.

'How did you know?' asked Little Bear.

Old Bear was just about to tell everyone to go back to sleep when there was an even louder *Whooo*. This time it came from the other side of the room.

He reached over and turned on the bedside light. 'I'm sure it's just the wind under the door,' he said, 'but I'd better go and see.' He slid down from the bed, rummaged in the drawer for the torch, and set off to investigate.

While they were waiting for Old Bear to return, Bramwell showed the other toys how to make funny shadow pictures on the wall. Little Bear thought he'd made a really good rabbit shape until he realised that it *was* Rabbit!

So he tried an elephant shadow instead and Rabbit made a crocodile that could open and shut its mouth. The crocodile was just about to bite the elephant's trunk when Old Bear returned.

'I didn't see anything,' he said, 'but someone has been here. All the things we left out have been tidied and put away.'

'Well, wind doesn't tidy things up,' said Little Bear, 'but I suppose a *ghost* might. Let's all go together and have a look.'

The toys jumped down from the bed and tiptoed across the room, peering into corners and behind the furniture. Then they heard the *Whooo* right above their heads.

'That's it!' cried Little Bear. 'That's my noise. It's on top of the cupboard.'

'Noises aren't usually on their own,' muttered Duck. 'They come from something.'

A s he spoke, something white swooped down and landed beside the
   toys. 'Hallooo, everyone,' it said.
   Little Bear dived to safety behind Old Bear and they all stared in
amazement at a little white owl in a blue apron.

'Well, what are you all doing up in the night?' asked the owl. 'You're usually fast asleep.'

'We heard a sort of ghostly *Whooo* noise,' said Little Bear, peeping out from behind Old Bear.

'That was me,' said the owl. 'I always do it. That's why they call me Hoot.'

'I heard a thump, too,' said Little Bear.
'Ah, that was my nest falling down,' explained Hoot.

'Oh dear,' said Old Bear. 'Where was your nest?'

'Up there,' replied Hoot, waving a wing at the tall cupboard. 'Only now it's down there,' she said sadly, pointing at the floor.

'But why have we never seen you before?' asked Little Bear.

'Owls sleep during the day,' said Hoot, 'and they come out at night. *You* all do it the opposite way round. I was always careful not to wake you. Until my nest fell down,' she added.

The toys all followed Hoot over to the fallen nest. 'It's made of socks,' said Bramwell in surprise, picking up one that had fallen out. 'Are they in pairs?'

'Oh, *no!*' said Hoot, 'I only use odd ones. I find them lying around. Socks are perfect for a nest, nice and soft and warm.'

'I always wondered where they went,' said Little Bear. 'We've got a whole drawer full of socks that don't match. How will you get your nest back up, Hoot?'

Hoot pulled at the nest and a sock came away in her beak. 'I don't think I can,' she said, sadly. 'It will fall apart if I move it.'

'Does your nest just have to be round and warm and soft?' asked Little Bear.

'That's right,' said Hoot.

'Well,' said Little Bear, 'I know something that will make a really good nest.'

He rushed off with the torch and returned a few minutes later with an old woolly bobble hat. '*This* won't fall apart,' he said, climbing into the hat. 'And it's very cosy. You try it, Hoot.'

Hoot carefully lowered herself into the hat and snuggled down. 'Yes, it's lovely,' she said. 'Thank you, Little Bear, but I wonder if I'll be able to fly with it.'

Old Bear found a piece of string and gave it to Hoot. 'If you fly to your cupboard with this,' he explained, 'we'll tie the hat to the other end and you can pull it up.'

'Wonderful,' said Hoot, stepping out of the nest. 'I'll see you later.' Then, spreading her wings, she flew right up to the top of the cupboard with the end of the string in her beak.

Little Bear tied the other end of the string to the bobble hat and Hoot began to pull. Just as the hat was leaving the ground, Little Bear gave a big leap and clung to the bobble. Hoot tugged hard on the string and Little Bear and the bobble hat rose into the air.

H oot was too busy pulling to see what she was lifting up, so when
Little Bear's ears suddenly appeared at the top of the cupboard, she
nearly dropped the string in surprise. 'What *are* you doing?' she asked,
helping Little Bear up.

'I wanted to see what it was like up here,' said Little Bear.

'But how will you get down?' asked Hoot.

'Hmm, I didn't really think about that,' said
Little Bear.

'Well, if you could help me put my
new nest in place, I'll give you a
ride down on my back,' said
Hoot, kindly.

Little Bear helped Hoot find just the right spot for her new nest. Then he climbed onto Hoot's back and she walked to the edge of the cupboard.

'Hold on tight!' called Hoot, and with a big flap of her wings, she launched herself into the air.

'Look, I'm flying!' called Little Bear, managing a quick wave to the others. They flew once around the room, swooped low over the bed and then landed gently, right beside Old Bear.

'I'm hungry now,' said Hoot, as her passenger climbed down.
'But it's the middle of the night,' said Little Bear.

'Exactly,' said Hoot. 'Lunch time for owls!'

She flew off again and returned with her lunch – a little pile of cheese and crackers wrapped in a handkerchief.

'Oh, lovely!' cried Little Bear. 'A midnight feast!'

'I don't think there will be enough for all of you,' said Hoot, doubtfully, as she carefully unwrapped the parcel of food. 'I wasn't really expecting guests.'

'Don't worry,' said Old Bear. 'We don't usually eat in the middle of the night so nobody will be very hungry.'

'Um…I think I might be, just a little bit,' said Little Bear, staring at the crackers.

'Well, do join me,' said Hoot. 'It'll be nice to have company for lunch.'

Old Bear realised that the other toys were beginning to look very sleepy, so when all the food had been eaten, he said it was time to say good night to Hoot and go back to bed. 'I'm sure we'll see you another night,' he said.

'And we'll try not to be too noisy in the daytime,' said Rabbit, 'now we know that you're asleep.'

Little Bear was so tired and full, he had to be carried off to bed and very soon all the toys were tucked up and fast asleep.

In the morning, they found that Hoot had had a very busy night!
All the socks were hanging from the end of the bed and they'd been
sorted into pairs; the socks from Hoot's nest and the matching ones
from the sock drawer.

The toys looked up at the cupboard. 'Thank you, Hoot,' they whispered, 'and good night.'

They thought they heard a sleepy *Whooo*, but it might just have been the wind outside.

Old Bear and Friends by Jane Hissey in Red Fox

OLD BEAR
LITTLE BEAR'S TROUSERS
LITTLE BEAR LOST
JOLLY TALL
JOLLY SNOW
HOOT
RUFF

A Red Fox Book

Published by Random House Children's Books
20 Vauxhall Bridge Road, London SW1V 2SA

A division of Random House UK Ltd
London Melbourne Sydney Auckland
Johannesburg and agencies throughout the world

Copyright © Jane Hissey 1996

1 3 5 7 9 10 8 6 4 2

First published in Great Britain by Hutchinson Children's Books 1996
Red Fox edition 1998
This Red Fox edition 1999

Printed in Singapore

RANDOM HOUSE UK Limited Reg. No. 954009

ISBN 0 09 969421 2

Some
bestselling Red Fox
picture books

THE BIG ALFIE AND ANNIE ROSE STORYBOOK
by Shirley Hughes
OLD BEAR
by Jane Hissey
OI! GET OFF OUR TRAIN
by John Burningham
DON'T DO THAT!
by Tony Ross
NOT NOW, BERNARD
by David McKee
ALL JOIN IN
by Quentin Blake
THE WHALES' SONG
by Gary Blythe and Dyan Sheldon
JESUS' CHRISTMAS PARTY
by Nicholas Allan
THE PATCHWORK CAT
by Nicola Bayley and William Mayne
WILLY AND HUGH
by Anthony Browne
THE WINTER HEDGEHOG
by Ann and Reg Cartwright
A DARK, DARK TALE
by Ruth Brown
HARRY, THE DIRTY DOG
by Gene Zion and Margaret Bloy Graham
DR XARGLE'S BOOK OF EARTHLETS
by Jeanne Willis and Tony Ross
WHERE'S THE BABY?
by Pat Hutchins